KU-130-564

Look what I've got!

Anthony Browne

JM

Julia MacRae Books

A division of Franklin Watts

Copyright © 1980 by Anthony Browne
All rights reserved

First published in Great Britain 1980 by
Julia MacRae Books
A Division of Franklin Watts
12a Golden Square, London W1R 4BA;
and Franklin Watts Inc.
387 Park Avenue South, New York 10016

Browne, Anthony
  Look what I've got!
  I. Title
  823'.9'1J   PZ7.B81984

ISBN 0-86203-004-8 U.K. edition
SBN 531-04-118-2 U.S. edition

Reprinted 1983

Printed in Belgium

For James
and Alex

Sam went for a walk.

Jeremy came by on his new bicycle.

"Look what I've got!" said Jeremy.
"I bet you wish you had one."

"Just watch me."

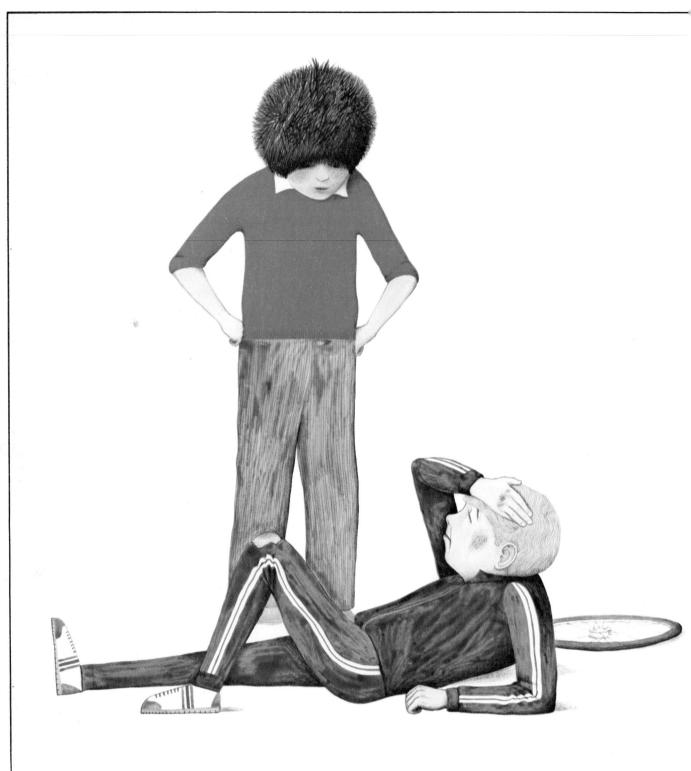

'Are you all right?" asked Sam.
Jeremy glared.

Sam went to the park.

Thud!

Jeremy was playing with his new football.
"Look what I've got!" he said. "I bet you
wish you had one."

They played football.

But Jeremy wasn't
very good.

Suddenly. . . .

Bang!

So Jeremy had
the ball . . .

. . . . Crash!

The park-keeper didn't seem very pleased.

Sam passed a shop. Jeremy came out
carrying an enormous bag of lollipops.

Look what I've got!" said Jeremy.
I bet you wish you had some."
He ate them all.

Jeremy sat down suddenly. . . .

Sam walked on, out of the town, towards the woods.

A gorilla leaped out at him.

Sam was terrified.

But it was Jeremy again.
"Look what I've got!" he said.
"I bet you wish you had one."

"Grrrrrrrrrr!"

But the old lady's dog was not frightened.

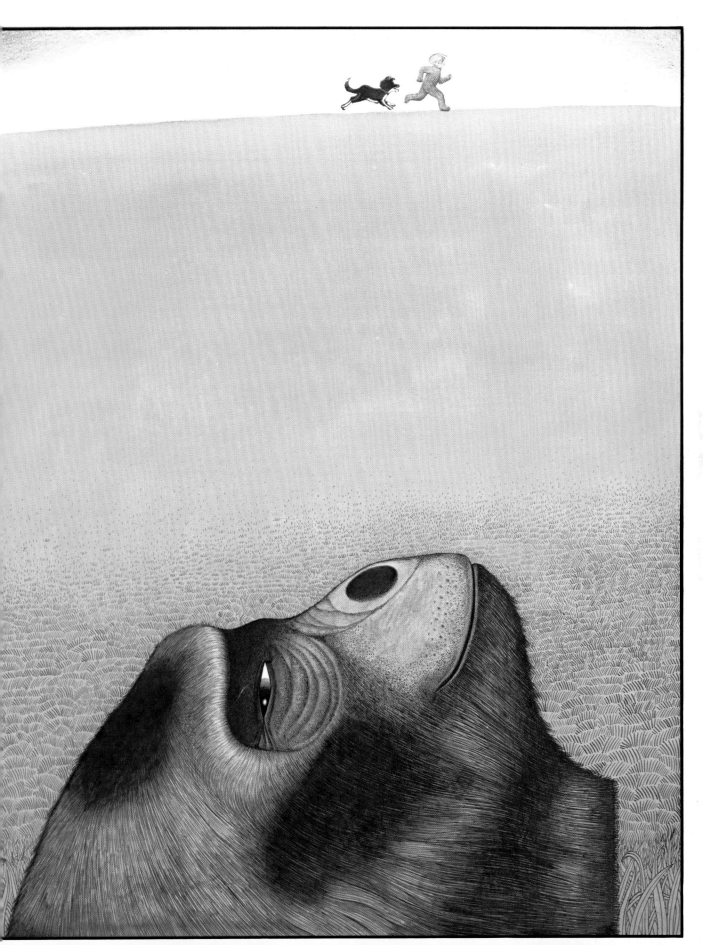

Sam stayed in the woods. Jeremy appeared.
"Look what I've got!" he said.
"I bet you wish you had one."

"No, not really," said Sam, and walked on.

But the wood was full of pirates.
They pounced on Jeremy.

The pirates made Jeremy walk the plank.

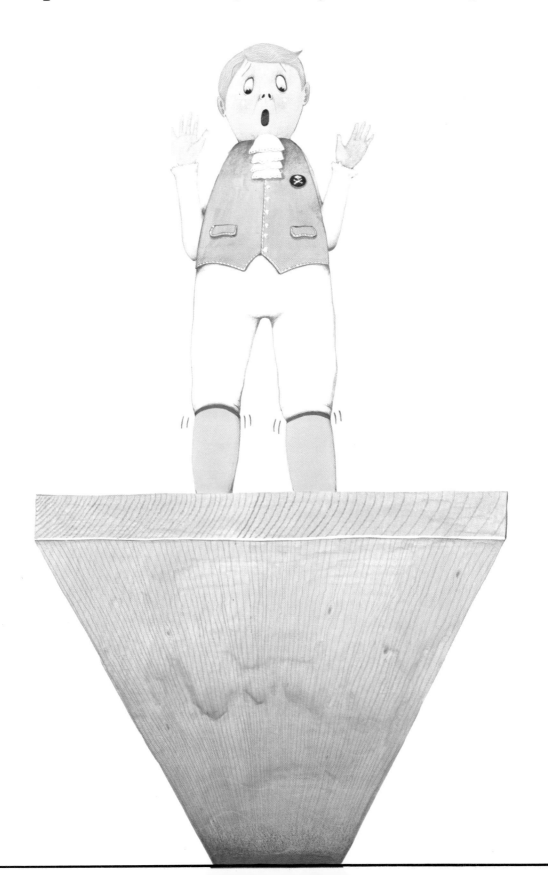

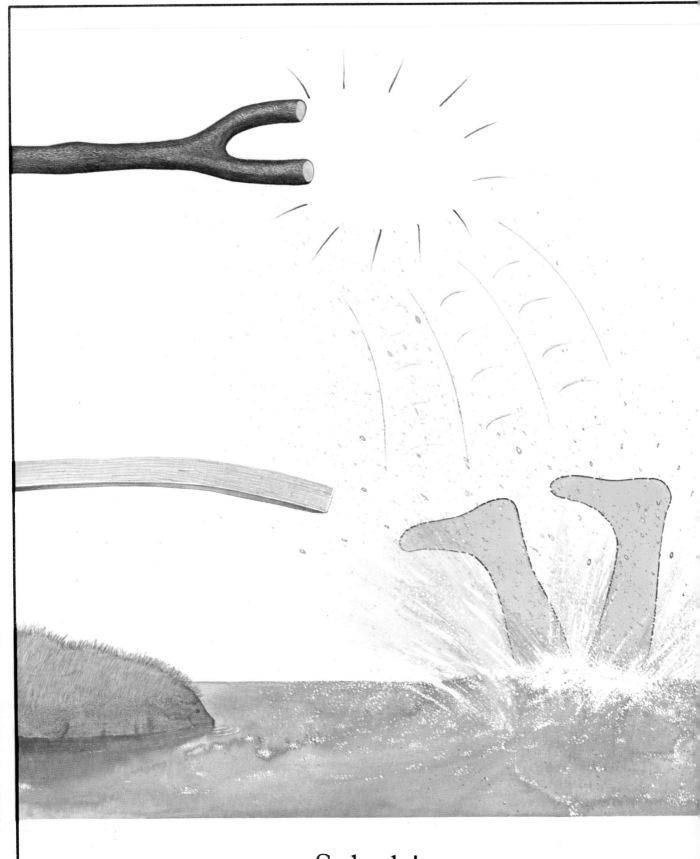

Splash!

Sam came back and pulled Jeremy out of
the water. "Hurry up," said Jeremy crossly.
"My dad's taking me to the zoo this afternoon.
I bet you wish you could come."

But Sam wasn't listening.